S0-AJM-252

AVON PUBLIC LIBRARY
BOX 977 / 200 BENCHMARK RD.
AVON, CO 81620

A919

31 00

INVENTIONS THAT CHANGED THE WORLD

THE LIGHT BULB

BY EMILY ROSE OACHS

BLASTOFF! DISCOVERY

Bellwether Media • Minneapolis, MN

**Blastoff! Discovery** launches
a new mission: reading to learn.
Filled with facts and features, each
book offers you an exciting new
world to explore!

This edition first published in 2019 by Bellwether Media, Inc.

No part of this publication may be reproduced in whole or in
part without written permission of the publisher.
For information regarding permission, write to Bellwether
Media, Inc., Attention: Permissions Department,
6012 Blue Circle Dr., Minnetonka, MN 55343.

Library of Congress Cataloging-in-Publication Data

Names: Oachs, Emily Rose, author.
Title: The Light Bulb / by Emily Rose Oachs.
Description: Minneapolis, MN : Bellwether Media, Inc., 2019.
   | Series: Blastoff! Discovery. Inventions that Changed the
   World | Includes bibliographical references and index. |
   Audience: Ages 7-13.
Identifiers: LCCN 2018040244 (print) | LCCN 2018041604
   (ebook) | ISBN 9781681037028 (ebook) | ISBN
   9781626179684 (hardcover : alk. paper)
   | ISBN 9781618915115 (pbk. : alk. paper)
Subjects: LCSH: Electric lighting–History–Juvenile literature.
   | Electric lamps–Juvenile literature. | Light bulbs–Juvenile
   literature. Classification: LCC TK4131 (ebook) | LCC
   TK4131 .O23 2019 (print) | DDC 621.32/6–dc23
LC record available at https://lccn.loc.gov/2018040244

Text copyright © 2019 by Bellwether Media, Inc. BLASTOFF!
DISCOVERY and associated logos are trademarks
and/or registered trademarks of Bellwether Media, Inc.
SCHOLASTIC, CHILDREN'S PRESS, and associated logos are
trademarks and/or registered trademarks of Scholastic Inc.,
557 Broadway, New York, NY 10012.

Editor: Betsy Rathburn    Designer: Josh Brink

Printed in the United States of America, North Mankato, MN

# TABLE OF CONTENTS

# READY TO LAND

An airplane circles a large city. From the windows, the passengers see the lights of tall buildings. Far below, cars speed down city streets. It is almost time to land!

Lights **illuminate** the dimly lit cabin, and passengers begin to gather their things. Seatbelt lights flash on above their heads. The passengers prepare for landing.

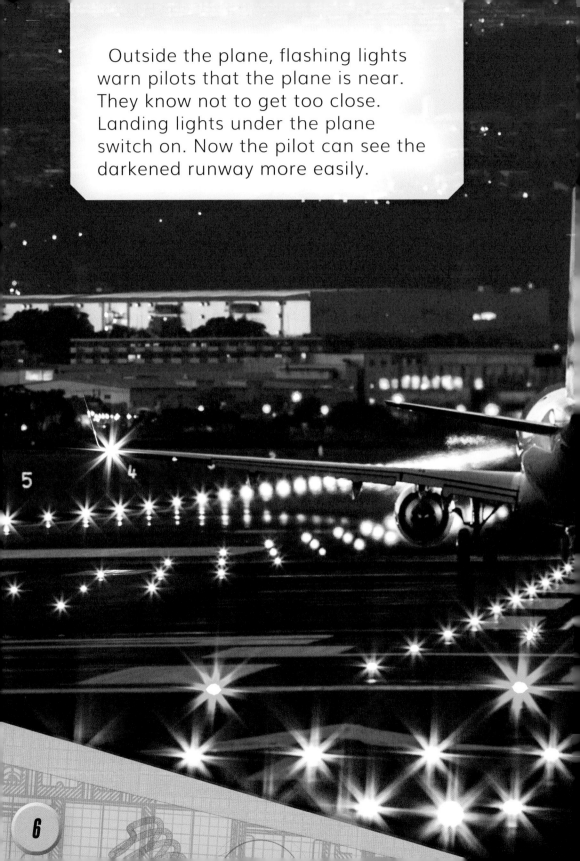

Outside the plane, flashing lights warn pilots that the plane is near. They know not to get too close. Landing lights under the plane switch on. Now the pilot can see the darkened runway more easily.

Finally, it is time to land. The pilot eases the plane down the runway. Perfect landing! Soon, it is time to leave the plane. Bright signs tell passengers where to go.
Light bulbs kept the passengers safe and comfortable!

# BRILLIANT IDEAS

Before light bulbs, people lit their homes with candles and gas lamps. But these could be dim, dangerous, and dirty. In the early 1800s, inventors worked to create electric lights. Within 100 years, light bulbs brought light into the night!

**Humphry Davy**

## DID YOU KNOW?

Moon towers once lit many cities around the world. These were tall towers with arc lamps at the top. The only moon towers still in use today are in Austin, Texas!

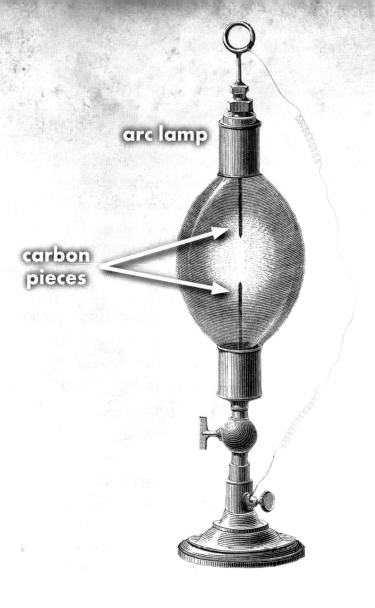

**arc lamp**

**carbon pieces**

The first electric light came in the early 1800s. Humphry Davy connected two pieces of **carbon** to a battery. It created a small light between the carbon pieces. This was an early **arc lamp**. By the end of the century, arc lamps lit the streets of Paris and other major cities!

Many people worked to create the first electric light bulb for homes. In 1835, James Bowman Lindsay introduced the first **incandescent** light bulb. Frederick de Moleyns **patented** this new bulb six years later.

These early light bulbs were **inefficient**, short-lived, and costly to build. Incandescent light bulbs created by Joseph Swan and Thomas Edison in 1879 overcame these issues. Their **filaments** were made of carbon that made the bulbs burn longer. Eventually, Edison created a bulb with a life span of 1,200 hours!

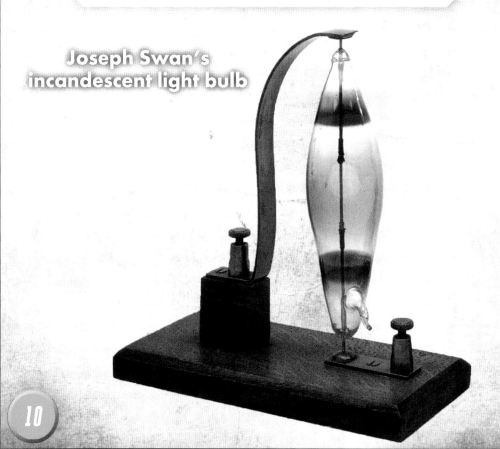

Joseph Swan's incandescent light bulb

# THOMAS EDISON

**Born:** February 11, 1847, in Milan, Ohio

**Background:** Inventor with little formal education who held a record 1,093 patents and whose inventions included the phonograph and the movie camera

**Light Bulb Invented:** first practical incandescent bulb

**Year Invented:** 1879

**Idea Development:** Edison bought patents for incandescent light bulbs from other inventors. This allowed him to build on their designs. He also worked hard testing thousands of different materials to be the bulb's filament. He eventually settled on carbon, which made his bulbs last longer than earlier designs.

# LIGHTS IN THE NIGHT

Inside Edison's new bulb, wires connected to a thin carbon filament. Electricity traveling through the wires heated the filament to make it glow. Later, inventors experimented with different filament materials. In 1906, General Electric patented the first bulb with a **tungsten** filament. Light bulbs began burning brighter than ever before!

Each fragile bulb was a **vacuum**. With no air inside the bulb, the filament burned longer. In 1913, Irving Langmuir added **nitrogen** to light bulbs. This gas gave bulbs even longer life spans!

# INCANDESCENT LIGHT BULB

Electricity flows through the wires to the filament. When electricity reaches the filament, the filament heats up and begins to glow.

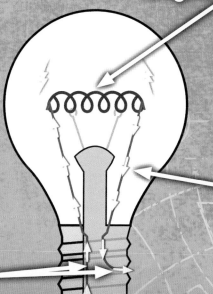

tungsten filament

electricity

wires

## DID YOU KNOW?

Today's bulbs still use tungsten filaments more than 100 years after their introduction!

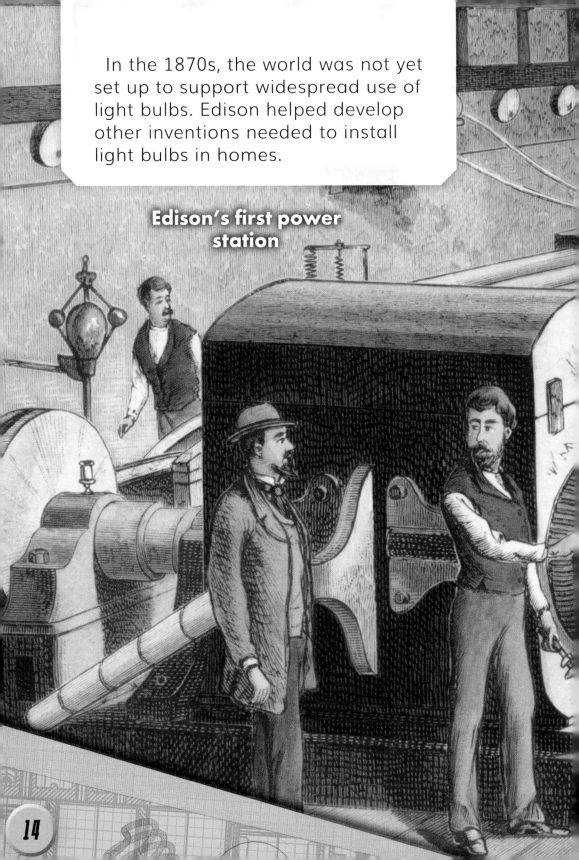

In the 1870s, the world was not yet set up to support widespread use of light bulbs. Edison helped develop other inventions needed to install light bulbs in homes.

**Edison's first power station**

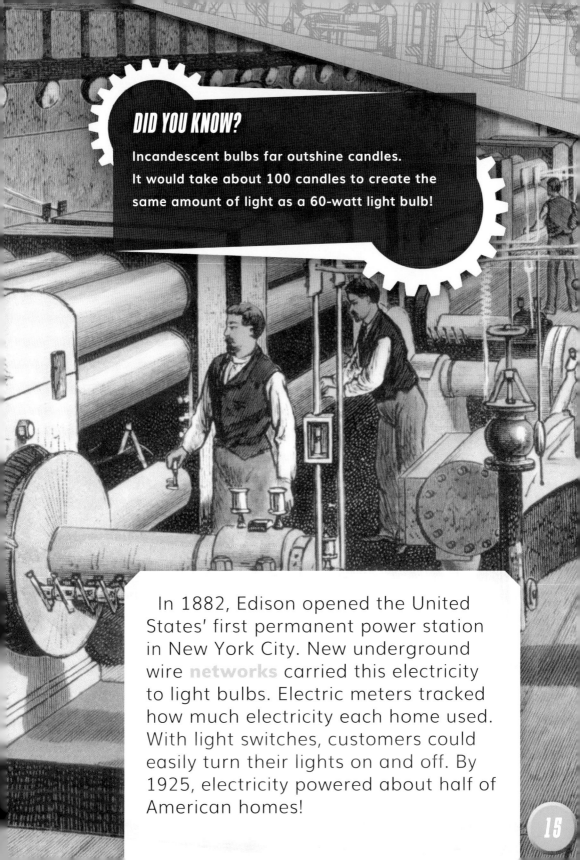

**DID YOU KNOW?**

Incandescent bulbs far outshine candles. It would take about 100 candles to create the same amount of light as a 60-watt light bulb!

In 1882, Edison opened the United States' first permanent power station in New York City. New underground wire **networks** carried this electricity to light bulbs. Electric meters tracked how much electricity each home used. With light switches, customers could easily turn their lights on and off. By 1925, electricity powered about half of American homes!

**fluorescent lamp**

By 1940, the longer-lasting fluorescent lamp was on the market. Inside its tube-shaped bulb, electricity passed through mercury gas. This created ultraviolet (UV) light. The bulb's phosphor coating changed the UV light into visible white light.

Soon, fluorescent bulbs lit hospitals, office buildings, shops, and schools. In 1976, Edward Hammer found a way to coil the fluorescent bulbs. These new compact fluorescent bulbs (CFLs) were much smaller. People could more easily use them in their homes.

compact fluorescent bulb

**Light-emitting diode** (LED) lights came in 1962. They created light when electricity passed through materials called **semiconductors**. This new lighting was highly efficient. It began to appear in many places, such as calculators and traffic signals.

# DID YOU KNOW?

Some companies have begun to pair LEDs with advanced computer technology. Now, people no longer need a switch to turn on lights. All they need is a smartphone app to light a room!

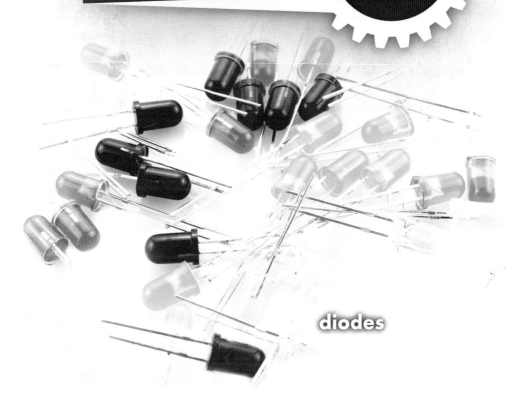

diodes

Advances in technology later brought organic light-emitting diode (OLED) lights to the market. These tiny bulbs release bright light. They are perfect for lighting television and computer displays. Today, researchers are creating new ways for OLEDs to light homes.

# CREATING THE MODERN WORLD

In time, the light bulb's invention had vast impacts. People were no longer bound to the sun's schedule. With electric lights, people could stay awake hours past sunset or rise long before dawn. Life became safer as people stopped burning candles for light at night.

The way people socialized and spent their free time changed. Restaurants were open late at night. Sporting events could take place after dark. Modern cities began to fill with bright lights!

The light bulb helped electrify homes. With electric lights came power stations and electrical wiring. Other electrical appliances, such as refrigerators and irons, came along later. Earlier wiring for electric light bulbs meant these appliances could easily be installed in homes. Soon, electricity became central to everyday life.

The electric light also lengthened workdays. Factories could run every hour of the day. Companies added overnight shifts. Now, they could get more work done!

power station

## LED LIGHT BULB

**Inventor's Name:** Nick Holonyak, Jr.

**Year of Release:** 1962

**Uses:** The efficiency and long life span of LED lights make these bulbs popular to use. These lights appear in many places, including in traffic signals, bicycle lights, car headlights and brake lights, watches, and television remotes. They are also used as indicator lights on calculators and other machines. More recently, LED light bulbs for use in homes and offices have come on the market.

### DID YOU KNOW?

Some LED bulbs have a life span of more than 50,000 hours. That means they can burn for more than five years straight!

Even building designs changed with the introduction of light bulbs. Some buildings had fewer windows. There was less of a need for sunlight to illuminate a room.

## DID YOU KNOW?

Electric lights also paved the way for other inventions. Without light bulbs, there would be no movie projectors, televisions, or smartphones!

**light pollution**

Electric lights also brought some negative effects. The high use of energy in incandescent bulbs contributes to climate change. Mercury in fluorescent bulbs is harmful to humans and the environment. Animals may become confused when light pollution brightens the sky.

# A BRIGHT FUTURE

Many people think the future of light is in LEDs. They are safer for the environment than incandescent and fluorescent lights. They are also much more efficient.

**LED bulb**

**incandescent bulb**

**LED lights**

Experts believe LED and OLED lights may also bring a new look to the light bulb. Rather than glass bulbs, thin panels of LEDs or OLEDs could bring light to homes and businesses. Like early incandescent bulbs, these LEDs and OLEDs will light the way to the future!

# LIGHT BULB TIMELINE

## 1801
Humphry Davy creates the first incandescent light

## 1880
Edison begins using a carbonized bamboo filament for 1,200 hours of light

## 1879
Thomas Edison patents the first practical incandescent light bulb

## 1882
The first American power station opens in New York City

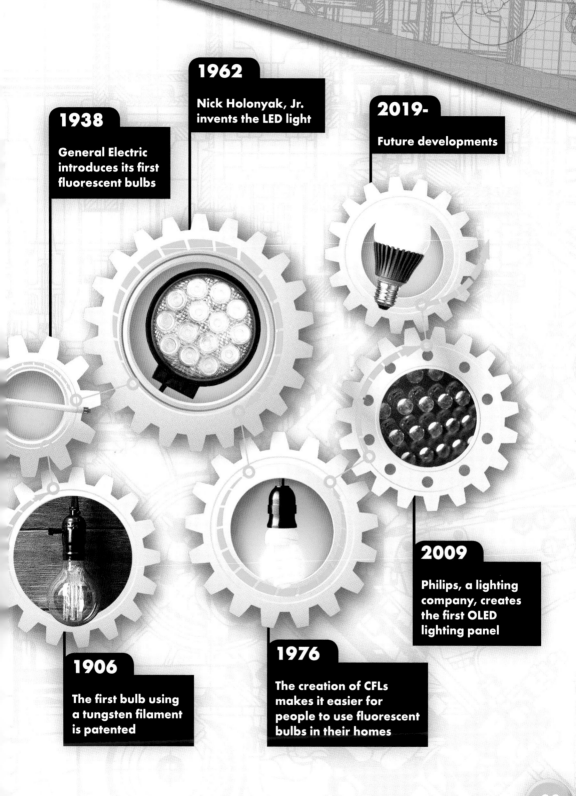

**1938**

General Electric introduces its first fluorescent bulbs

**1962**

Nick Holonyak, Jr. invents the LED light

**2019-**

Future developments

**2009**

Philips, a lighting company, creates the first OLED lighting panel

**1906**

The first bulb using a tungsten filament is patented

**1976**

The creation of CFLs makes it easier for people to use fluorescent bulbs in their homes

# GLOSSARY

**arc lamp**—a type of bulb that creates light when electricity travels through the air between two electrodes

**carbon**—a natural element found in common materials such as coal

**climate change**—a human-caused change in Earth's weather that leads to warming temperatures

**environment**—the natural surroundings

**filaments**—thin pieces of material that glow when electricity travels through them

**fluorescent lamp**—a type of bulb that produces light when electricity passes through mercury in a phosphor-coated tube

**illuminate**—to light up

**incandescent**—releasing light after being heated up

**inefficient**—wasting energy

**light pollution**—illumination from electric lights that makes the stars and other objects in the night sky difficult to see

**light-emitting diode**—a type of light that is produced when electricity passes through semiconductors

**mercury**—a natural element whose liquid form is often used in thermometers

**networks**—groups of connected objects that operate together

**nitrogen**—a natural element found in all living things

**patented**—protected with a document that gives an inventor all rights to create and sell their invention

**phosphor**—a material that glows when ultraviolet light passes through it

**semiconductors**—types of materials that electricity can pass through

**tungsten**—a heavy metallic element

**ultraviolet**—a type of light that is invisible to the eye

**vacuum**—a space in which all the air has been sucked out

# TO LEARN MORE

## AT THE LIBRARY

Cimarusti, Nick. *Thomas Edison: Lighting a Revolution.* Huntington Beach, Calif.: Teacher Created Materials, Inc., 2019.

Hamen, Susan E. *Who Invented the Light Bulb?: Edison vs. Swan.* Minneapolis, Minn.: Lerner Publications, 2018.

Jackson, Demi. *How Does a Light Bulb Work?* New York, N.Y.: Gareth Stevens Publishing, 2016.

## ON THE WEB

# FACTSURFER

Factsurfer.com gives you a safe, fun way to find more information.

1. Go to www.factsurfer.com.

2. Enter "light bulb" into the search box.

3. Click the "Surf" button and select your book cover to see a list of related web sites.

# INDEX

The images in this book are reproduced through the courtesy of: mnowicki, front cover (center), pp. 23, 29 (LED light); actionvance, front cover (bottom); pisaphotography, p. 4; Cassiohabib, p. 5; beeboys, pp. 6-7; Science History Images/ Alamy, pp. 8, 10; Photo 12/ Alamy, p. 9; Everett Historical, pp. 11 (left), 14-15, 28 (power station); sspl/ Getty Images, p. 11 (right); Ezume Images, p. 12; Olegro, p. 13 (lightning bolt); Prapat Aowsakorn, p. 16; Iakov Filimonov, p. 17; alice-photo, p. 18; HelloRF Zcool, p. 19; ElenaChaykinaPhotography, p. 20; Let Go Media, p. 21; Jenoche, p. 22; Krasowit, p. 23 (right); 06photo, p. 24; EpicStockMedia, p. 25; BlurryMe, p. 26; Michael Dechev, p. 27; Kelson/ Wikipedia, p. 28 (Humphry Davy); Daderot (bamboo filament bulb); Alex.D/ Wikipedia, p. 28 (incandescent bulb); Africa Studio, p. 29 (tungsten filmanet bulb); Leonid Andronov, p. 29 (fluorescent bulb); n_defender, p. 29 (LED lights); Chones, p. 29 (CFL bulb); photokup, p. 29 (OLED panel).

AVON PUBLIC LIBRARY
BOX 977 / 200 BENCHMARK RD.
AVON, CO 81620